It's too dark!

For Mom & Dad, who showed me the stars and how to work hard to reach them.

DIAL BOOKS FOR YOUNG READERS
An imprint of Penguin Random House LLC, New York

First published in the United States of America by Dial Books for Young Readers, an imprint of Penguin Random House LLC, 2022

Dial & colophon are registered trademarks of Penguin Random House LLC. Visit us online at penguinrandomhouse.com.
Library of Congress Cataloging-in-Publication Data is available. Manufactured in China • ISBN 9780593324387

10 9 8 7 6 5 4 3 2 1
HH

Design by Jennifer Kelly
Text handlettered by Vanessa Roeder

The Stack

Vanessa Roeder

Dial Books for Young Readers

It started with a single chair.

On it, Luna reached up high...

But couldn't quite get there.

Even with a stepping stool
it was a tad too low.

She ran away and then returned
with twenty books in tow.

Luna stacked them,

ONE

BY

ONE,

with vigilance and care,

and when she climbed atop the stack
she started to despair.

Her quest seemed insurmountable.
She had to think much bigger.

She planned
a complicated
scheme
to execute
with vigor.

Atop the books
she placed her bed,
set upright
on its end.

Next she tossed a
clawfoot tub
that held her
tallest friend.

Luna piled on
stacks of plates.
Her mother's
finest set.

Then

she launched

her neighbor's

house.

But she couldn't reach just yet.

An elephant,

a humpback whale,

her grandpa's station wagon . . .

She flung a princess in a tower...

She even chucked the dragon.

I think I'm airsick.

FINALLY atop
the beast
she heaved a
pirate ship.

She grabbed a pack,
a jar, a snack
and started
on her trip.

She
climbed
and
clambered

up
she
went

with all her
strength
and might.

She scaled the great colossal stack

up to its highest height.

Carefully she perched on top and opened up the jar.

Luna stood
on tippy-toe
to reach
a single star.

She placed
the twinkling
star inside
and screwed
the lid on
tight.

With
the
prize

clutched
in her
arms

she
made
her
downward
flight.

Back inside her room that night
the gleaming starlight spread.

She glanced around her room and wished...

she hadn't tossed her bed.

TURN LEFT AT THE ELEPHANT
ZZZZZZ

But Luna didn't mind so much.

She had her light instead.

Sweet dreams.